MEGALODON

ERIC S BROWN

SEVERED PRESS
Hobart Tasmania

MEGALODON

ISBN: 978-1-925342-36-9

MEGALODON

The Twin City was your standard class, smaller fishing rig. Harold's father had owned her for a decade now and was rather proud of her. Not every fisherman could afford to fully own their boat in these continually growing darker economic times. Both his grandfather and father were fishermen before him. Sometimes, he felt like the family legacy was more a curse than a blessing. Harold loved the sea but until his father's heart attack last year, he honestly hadn't even considered taking over the family business.

He sat at the Twin City's helm, watching the waves roll about through her forward window. The night was a peaceful one. Most of the crew was asleep and getting ready for another hard day of work come the morning. So far, they were well ahead of their quota and Harold wanted to keep it that way. He took a long drag from the cigarette he held and blew the smoke up at the ceiling as he leaned back in his seat.

As he did, a red light began to flash on the helm. It was the proximity alarm. Harold frowned. He knew this part of the ocean well. There shouldn't be anything in the area large enough to be a threat to the ship. Springing forward, he quickly ground out his cigarette on the helm itself and started to check the sonar screen. He froze though as he saw the massive fin rising up out of the water ahead of the Twin City. The fin appeared to be as tall as the Twin City was.

He blinked and rubbed at his tired eyes, sure that he had to be hallucinating. When he opened his eyes again, the fin was gone.

With a sigh of relief, Harold slumped back into his seat and began to relax. As he did so, he noticed the proximity alarm was still flashing. *What in the devil?* He thought.

Then without warning, something rammed into the Twin City. It struck her with the force of a volley of torpedoes all detonating at once. Her hull folded inward as her engines blew below her decks. Harold never even had time to scream. The Twin City blossomed into a ball of fire that lit the night.

Several miles away, on the deck of the military vessel, the USS Newton, Dr. David Powell smiled. "See Captain," he gloated, "I told you she wouldn't have any trouble with a target that size. Now take us home to the platform. There's a lot of work ahead of us yet."

****

Dr. Leia Carpenter sat in the rear of the transport chopper as it sped southward through the increasingly dark clouds. The pilot had expressed concerns about reaching the new home of the "Sonar 1" project before the approaching storm overtook them. In fact, he hadn't wanted to make the trip at all. The powers that be, however, wouldn't accept "no" as an answer. They wanted Leia there as quickly as possible to analyze the data from Dr. Powell's supposed breakthrough.

By anyone's standards, Powell was a genius when

it came to sonar and aquatic life. No one could argue with that. Powell, despite his genius, was also highly unliked in the world of politics. He was an eccentric sort who too often spoke the truth as he saw it. Add to this that Powell often wasn't able to see the "big picture", his attention always narrowed on his work, and the government had no choice but to have someone else confirm his data before ever presenting it to the boards that decided what funding the project would receive.

The importance of the Sonar 1 project was that of Alpha Level status and as thus, Leia had been torn away from her own work to confirm or debunk Powell's. The military hadn't even given her any kind of real notice. They had just shown up off the coast of Brazil and stolen her away from her team during the night. She was more than a bit ticked off about that but what could she do?

Colonel Martin Wilson and *his* team shared the rear of the chopper with her. She could feel him staring at her but refused to look up and meet his eyes. Instead, she kept her own gaze glued to the screen of the data pad she held in her hands, trying to be as ready as she could for when she met Dr. Powell. Besides, all the grunts accompanying Wilson put her ill at ease. Each of them were armed to the teeth and looked more like they should be heading off into battle than escorting an egghead like her to a remote oceanic platform.

Leia understood the potential military applications of the work on board Sonar 1 well enough whether she approved of them or not. Still, the presence of the colonel and his goons struck her as more than a little over the top.

"Dr. Carpenter," Colonel Wilson called to her through the comlink inside the helmet she wore. His voice came over a private channel and not the general one shared by the group. "We'll be touching down in five."

"Thank you," she answered politely, trying to keep her own voice from showing how she really felt about her current situation, not that the colonel would have cared. He had his orders and she had hers.

Leia shutdown her data pad. "Mind if I move up front so I can get a look at the overall platform as we're landing?"

Wilson barked a few orders over the com-net and the co-pilot entered the chopper's rear compartment, motioning for Leia to move up and take his place.

She handed Wilson her data pad as she passed him. "Make sure this is safe."

Wilson shot her a feral grin. "Count on it. That's part of my job, ma'am."

The colonel was a small man and reminded Leia of a weasel. A very, very deadly weasel but a weasel none the less. He had a slimy edge to him and the sleek, well-carved shape of his angular features emphasized it.

The pilot was so focused on the weather and keeping the helicopter on course that he didn't even seem to notice Leia as she slipped into the co-pilot seat beside him. Leia wasn't offended by this. It actually comforted her.

He was at least a decade younger than the colonel

was, maybe in his later twenties. The nametag on his uniform read Stevens. Leia didn't dare speak to him. The last thing he needed with the storm closing in on them and beginning to overtake the helicopter was someone like her asking a lot of stupid questions.

Leia turned her attention to the platform in the distance. It was massive. Much larger than an oilrig and perhaps the largest oceanic facility she had ever seen. It was square in its overall shape and in its center was a well-lit tower that stretched upwards towards the dark clouds.

Home, she thought bitterly. And it would be her home for the next several weeks as she plowed through Dr. Powell's work. No contact, except through proper and authorized channels, with the outside world was going to be allowed. She had been cut off from the world before. Things like that was merely a part of her job when it came right down to it, but every time she headed into a "need to know only" type area, she got the jitters. Leia blamed her love of horror films for this. Too many bad things could happen to people who were isolated and essentially stranded in the middle of nowhere.

As the helicopter got closer to the platform, Leia could see several small naval vessels around it.

They were very much like the old Cyclone class but much smaller. A few tiny figures of their crews moved about the decks preparing the ships for the coming storm. Leia did not fail to notice that all of them were military vessels. She imagined they were tasked as much with protecting the Sonar 1 facility as much as they were with assisting Dr. Powell.

"Ma'am," the pilot said to her, "if you wouldn't mind returning to the rear, we're about to touchdown."

Leia smiled at him. She knew what he really meant was that *the weather was going to make this tricky enough. Would you be so kind as to get the heck out of my way?*

"Sure thing," she answered, exiting the copter's pilot compartment as she and the co-pilot traded places once more.

"You see all you need to?" Colonel Wilson smirked, handing her data pad to her.

Leia nodded. She took her seat and strapped in. From seeing how Steven was handling the rough weather on as the copter closed on the base, she had faith he would get them down just fine, but there was no point in taking chances.

Less than three minutes later, the copter sat on the landing pad of the Sonar 1 platform. Colonel Wilson's men filed out of the bird first, establishing a perimeter around it. Leia couldn't help but think how ridiculous that was, but she kept that feeling to herself. She slipped a plastic carrying bag over her data pad before following Colonel Wilson into the rain. They were the last to disembark from the helicopter except for the two pilots who were still busy shutting down its systems.

The rain was pouring as the two of them raced across the landing pad and into the platform's interior structure. It was a cold rain. The falling drops stabbed Leia's exposed skin, causing her to flinch each time one hit her.

The run was a short one, but that didn't stop them from getting drenched. As soon as they were through the door, Leia shook herself, flinging water onto the walls of the corridor. She was shivering as she removed her data pad from the soaked plastic covering it. Seeing that it was okay, she noticed they weren't alone in the corridor.

Two armed people, one man and one woman, who appeared to be part of the Platform's security team were already waiting on them alongside an older man in a well used, white lab coat. She didn't recognize the man in the lab coat. She had seen photos and news footage of Dr. Powell and she knew it wasn't he. It would be just like Powell to send a flunky to meet them in his place based on what she had heard of the good doctor.

The older man stepped forward, extending his hand to her. "Welcome to Sonar 1, Dr. Carpenter," he said.

Leia accepted his hand and shook it.

"Gregory," Colonel Wilson nodded at the armed man. The man nodded back at him but said nothing. Leia saw that the two of them clearly knew each other.

"Where's Dr. Powell?" Leia asked.

The older man shrugged. "I'm afraid that Dr. Powell's work keeps him rather busy. I'm Dr. Robert Jenkins, the Sonar 1 platform's resident Marine Biologist. My role here is limited to that of a consultant on an as needed basis with Dr. Powell. As thus, I doubt our paths will cross very much," he paused, gesturing at the guards with him, "This is

Chief Gregory Shoyer, and his associate Melinda Watson. They head up the platform's internal security division. If you have need of anything, don't hesitate to ask one of them."

Neither Gregory nor Melinda offered her anything more than an appraising stare. Nonetheless, Leia nodded a greeting at them.

"Melinda," Jenkins ordered, "If you would be so kind as to show Dr. Carpenter to her quarters. I am sure she would like to get settled and changed as quickly as possible."

"This way, ma'am," Melinda said, leading the two of them deeper into the platform. Leia stole a glance over her shoulder as they went. Colonel Wilson and Gregory remained standing with Dr. Jenkins, talking, as the colonel's men began to come inside from the rain through the still open exterior doorway.

Melinda led Leia around a bend in the corridor. "Dr. Powell is rather eager to meet you, ma'am."

Right, Leia thought, *And that's why he was here waiting for me himself.*

"I would think so seeing as how the fate of his continued funding for this operation hinges on the report I make," Leia pretended to agree. Besides, adding a degree of importance to her standing when dealing with folks like Melinda never hurt.

"I don't know about all that, ma'am. I just know he hasn't stopped talking about you since he was informed of your pending arrival," Melinda answered.

The maze of corridors stretched on and on as they continued walking.

"Just how big is this place?" Leia finally asked.

"Much larger than it appears from the outside," Melinda shrugged. "Most of the primary facility structure is underneath the surface platform where you landed."

Melinda must have anticipated her next question because she continued on, "There are almost two dozen staff members, counting security personnel such as myself, who live permanently aboard the platform. The ships you must have seen on your approach have their own crews, of course."

"You'll excuse me if all this is a bit much to take in," Leia frowned. "I'm no stranger to high clearance level projects but this. . ."

"Is impressive," Melinda finished for her with a smirk on her face.

"That's one way to put it," Leia wiped a strand of her wet hair back into place from where it had fallen down into her eyes.

"The work Dr. Powell is doing here is going to change the world." Melinda came to a stop outside of a doorway to their right. "This is where you'll be staying, ma'am."

Melinda handed her a key card. "As with many doors inside the platform, this has a dual mechanism lock. This card, along with a quick DNA scan the platform's AI runs as you slide it, will unlock the door."

Leia accepted the card and used it to open the door to her quarters. Inside, there was only a single, small bunk, a work desk in the room's center, and a bath that had no door of its own. She could see the toiletries and shower through the open doorway from where she stood.

"I'll leave you to it then," Melinda announced. "Either Gregory or one the colonel's men will be by shortly with your bags. Once you connect your data pad to the platform's net, you should be able to download any maps you need, so getting lost shouldn't be a problem."

Melinda started to leave but turned abruptly back towards Leia, "Oh, and Dr. Powell requests that you join him as promptly as possible in his personal lab."

"I'll do things as quickly as I can," Leia assured her and then Melinda was gone.

****

Within five minutes, her two small bags had arrived. A private named Berkman delivered them to her and left as promptly as he had arrived. Leia changed quickly, not bothering to unpack the rest of the things she had brought with her. She fired up her data pad and downloaded several maps of the platform's interior. The level of clearance she had been granted made logging onto the platform's net easy. Once she finished, she ventured out bravely, data pad in hand, into the winding maze of corridors outside her quarters.

With Dr. Powell waiting on her, there was no time to study the maps she downloaded in great detail. She located Powell's personal lab on the map that she currently had open on the data pad's screen and set out to find it.

The path her data pad provided took her across the level she was on and down two more before she reached the lab. To her surprise, the lab's door slid open as she approached it. She entered, stopping just inside it. The walls of the lab were covered in wide assortment of posters ranging from slogans like "The Truth is out there" to a giant sized white number 4 set inside a circle of white against a blue background. The largest and most striking poster was one of a comic book hero in rather revealing attire, who wore a golden lasso that dangled, coiled up, from the side of her waist. The room contained multiple work areas, some with a more chemistry slant, and others with a more engineering one. The one in the center of the room though contained a large microscope with a large stack of slides sitting beside it on its left side. On the work area's right side was a massive monitor on which was displayed the Sonar 1's project logo-a jagged lightning bolt smashing through a battleship.

Dr. Powell sat at the central work area, his back towards the doorway she stood in. His head bobbed as if in time to music.

"Dr. Powell?" Leia called to him, raising her voice in the hope that he would hear her over whatever he was listening to.

He spun around in his chair, jerking out the pair of ear buds he wore. His lips were spread wide in a happy smile. "Ah, Dr. Carpenter," he laughed, "I see you've arrived safely at last!"

Dr. Powell bounded from his seat, springing towards her as if to embrace her. Leia took a cautious step back. He noticed her uncomfortableness in the moment, lowering his arms. "It's my sincere pleasure to meet you." He beamed like an over eager kid buzzing on his third can of

Redbull. "I must confess that, given the nasty weather, I was concerned. The storm that's rolling in on Sonar 1 is a record breaker for this region or so I am told."

Powell was even more strikingly young for a man of his accomplishments in person than he appeared in his file. He couldn't be more than thirty or thirty one years old, tops. Yet, he held more degrees in various areas than Leia could remember off the top of her head. His eyes were a deep shade of blue and his teeth overly white. Everything about the man screamed, "Nerd." With his looks, he would have been just at home at comic con as he appeared in his lab. The décor of his lab confirmed that. In addition to the posters on the lab walls, scattered stacks of well-read comics lay in random places about the lab in an absentminded nature. Not to say the place was messy. It was merely chaotic in its arrangement.

"It's good to meet you as well, sir." Leia did her best to return his enthusiasm.

"I know exactly what you're thinking," he waggled a finger at her.

"And that would be?" Leia asked out of curiosity.

"How does a kid like me warrant all this cloak and dagger stuff?" Dr. Powell's smile grew even wider as he spoke. "I mean, there are quite a lot of guys with guns running about this place making sure me and my work are safe."

When Leia said nothing, he continued. "I bet they told you this project was related to Sonar tech. Am I right?"

"Isn't it?" Leia frowned.

"Not at all, my dear, not at all; the sonar bit is just a cover for my real work," Dr. Powell admitted.

"Then do you mind if I ask why I am here?"

"You're here, young lady. . ." Dr. Powell paused as Leia's expression turned angry. "You don't mind that I called you that, do you? If so, please forgive me. I'm just excited."

"You were saying your work has nothing to do with sonar tech," Leia urged him on.

"Oh yes. Sorry. I do tend to forget myself sometimes. As I was saying, my work is related to sonar tech, yes, but that's not what it is."

Dr. Powell walked over to a mini-fridge in the corner of the lab and produced two sodas from it. He offered her one. Leia took it without argument, though she didn't open her can.

"Please call me Dave," he told her. "Despite all the protocols that have to be obeyed on this platform, we're not big on formality with those who are part of our team."

Dave sighed, chugged half of his Dr. Pepper down in a single gulp, and then sat the can aside.

"I realize your current work is related to the effect of sonar transmission on marine life, Dr. Carpenter, but that was not always the case. In the beginning of your career, you were very deeply involved with a whole other sort of research, were you not?"

"Sharks." Her breath caught as she said the word. "You're experimenting with sharks."

"No, Dr. Carpenter. I am experimenting on *the* shark. The mother of all sharks if you will," Dave giggled.

Leia's eyes bugged. "Don't tell me you've found. . ."

"A Megalodon, Dr. Carpenter. One so massive and abnormal you wouldn't believe it until you see her yourself."

****

Colonel Wilson sat on the edge of Gregory's bunk. The security leader sat across the small room from him in its only chair. The sparse quarters allowed no room for any other seats. Weeks had passed since Wilson had set foot aboard the Sonar 1 Platform and the two men had much to catch up on.

Wilson left the mundane duties of getting his men settled and their duties assigned to his second in command before coming here. He watched as Gregory poured them both a glass from a bottle of aged scotch.

"It's good to have you on board again, sir," Gregory said, handing Wilson his glass.

"Has there been any trouble since I left?"

"Nothing I couldn't handle. Powell is like a freak on cocaine but a manageable one if you know how to handle him. Captain Herc has given me some issues though. As Powell's experiments have gotten, how can I say this, *more involved,* Herc has balked at some of the orders Powell has given him."

"I can understand why," Wilson grunted. "In Herc's place, I might do the same. Doesn't change anything though. Orders are orders."

"Now that you're back, I figure Herc will toe the line," Gregory lifted his glass in Wilson's direction

14

before downing its contents.

"He had better," Wilson said, his tone serious and dark.

Wilson took a sip from his own drink. "How's Lightning holding up?"

Any sincere good humor Gregory had been showing disappeared instantly.

"She's becoming more aggressive every day. Worse, she is continuing to draw a crowd."

"That was always a concern." Wilson rubbed at his cheeks with the fingers of his free hand. "Not much we can do about that unless we kill them."

"You have the authority to order that no matter what the good doctor says," Gregory pointed out. "I wouldn't though. We had no choice but to thin their numbers to a more tolerable level while you were away in DC. It drove Lightning crazy. Took us days to calm her down."

"I still don't understand that," Wilson confessed. "It just doesn't make any sense. There's no reason the crowd she's been drawing should matter to her at all."

"Maybe it's some side effect of Powell messing around with her head like he is."

"Who knows?" Wilson shook his head. "It's Powell's job to figure out crap like that. All we need to make sure of is that our goal here is met. The powers that be have sunk too much into this project for us to come up empty handed."

"Heard you had a rough trip coming in this time," Gregory changed the subject.

"I've had worse," Wilson sat his drink onto the

floor next to his feet. "This platform was designed to stand up to Lightning herself. A hurricane, even one like this, isn't going to be an issue to us beyond slowing down Powell's work."

"Herc is pretty on about it."

"The ships under his command can take this weather too," Wilson reminded Gregory. "If they couldn't, they wouldn't be stationed here."

"Tell him that," Gregory snorted, then became serious again. "This Dr. Carpenter you brought, can we trust her?"

"No," Wilson answered freely, "but Powell claims to need her so we don't have much choice in the matter."

"Accidents on Sonar Platform 1 have happened before," Gregory said quietly.

"Let's hope it doesn't come to that," Wilson got to his feet. "Thanks for the drink. I suppose I better go touch base with Herc before he throws a hissy fit though."

"Anytime, colonel," Gregory saluted.

****

Dave directed Leia to the microscope atop the workstation he had been sitting at when she entered. "Go on. Take a look and tell me what you see."

Leia's mind was reeling from his claim of having located a real, living Megalodon. Dave's hints that it had been captured and somehow tamed were even more staggering. She wanted more than anything to *see* it, but Dave insisted that she needed to understand his work better and what he was up to here at Sonar Platform 1 before taking her to it.

Reluctantly, Leia approached the microscope. She leaned over it with Dave watching her and peered at the slide he readied for her. Leia noticed at once that the cell on the slide must belong to the Megalodon Dave had mentioned. Something wasn't right about it though. How the cell functioned and appeared, as she looked closer at it was baffling. Then Leia noticed why. Inside the cell, something that clearly wasn't biologic in nature was moving about.

Leia looked up from the microscope at Dave. "Those things in the cell...you created them, didn't you?"

"Caught red handed," Dave grinned. "Those tiny little robotic things you see allow me to control Lightning to a degree."

"Lightning?" Leia asked, unable to draw any connection to the word from what she had just looked at. Then at once, she put two and two together. "You really do *have* a Megalodon and you named it Lightning?"

Dave sounded hurt as he answered, "I think Lightning sounds cool."

Leia stared at him.

"Okay, okay," Dave caved in. "There's a reason why she got that name. Two of them actually, but let's save those stories for later. What do you think of my tech?"

"I'm not an expert in nano-tech," Leia said, "How the heck should I know?"

"You are an expert when it comes to sharks and Megalodons though," Dave countered. "I was referring to how my tech interacts with the Megalodon's cell tissue and nucleus."

Leia started to lean over the microscope again, but Dave stopped her.

"No need to do that. I sent a file containing data on the interaction of my nano-tech and the Megalodon's bioelectrical brain energy to your pad. Take a glance at the file instead."

Leia powered on her data pad and opened the data. She read for a few moments while Dave waited patiently. Finally, she said, "There is some sort of feedback occurring between your tech and the Megalodon's brain."

"Yes," Dave said. "My nano-tech allows me to control the Megalodon to an extent as I said, but that's not all that's happening. There is a far greater energy output occurring from the Megalodon's brain than I can account for."

"You're right," Leia agreed. "At the level it is occurring, it will burn out your nanobots in a matter of weeks."

"And *that* is the primary reason you're here," Dave laid a hand on Leia's shoulder. "I need to know exactly what is transpiring and how to stop it."

"It'll take me some time to plow through all this," Leia answered honestly.

"I know," Dave nodded. "That is why I had them rush you here. The clock is ticking."

****

"Accept it, amigo," Mendez waved a hand at the raging storm outside the observation window. "We're grounded for the duration."

Stevens plopped into a chair beside the on duty radar operator, Timothy.

"Your partner is right, mate," Timothy told him. "That storm out there is only getting worse. You take off into it and you'll be coming down hard."

"I can't believe this crap," Stevens complained. "We were supposed to be in and out before the storm got here."

"As long as you've been flying for the Navy, buddy, you should be used to this kind of crap by now," Mendez walked over and smacked Steven's back. What's your problem anyway? We're essentially getting paid to sit on our butts."

Mendez was a rookie by Stevens' standards. This was only their third flight together. The two of them hadn't had time to fully get to know each other yet. Mendez was as competent a co-pilot as Stevens could ask for, but the man grated on his nerves.

"Look," Stevens said, "it's pretty dang clear that whatever is going on aboard this platform is high priority and dangerous. Sonar Platform 1 has *black op* written all over it. Personally, I like to keep as much distance as I can from stuff like that. I mean that sort of stuff has a tendency blow up in your face pretty quick."

Mendez lit up a smoke. Stevens noted that Timothy didn't call him on breaking regs, as Mendez puffed on it.

"Relax, amigo," Mendez assured him. "How long can this storm possibly last? We'll be out of here before you know. Just kick back and enjoy our time off, like I am."

"That lady you guys flew in was pretty hot," Timothy cut in. "What's she like?"

Stevens and Mendez both stared at Timothy with amused expressions.

"Down boy," Mendez laughed, flicking ash from his cigarette into a half empty coffee mug. "She's way out of your league."

Timothy's cheeks grew red with embarrassment.

"I will admit she *is* hot for a geek," Mendez took another drag on his smoke, turning serious. "You spoke with her, Stevens, so what ya think? She do-able or too cold and stuck up to waste energy making a move on?"

"You know as much about her as I do," Stevens protested. "According to what little we were told about her and what I overheard, she's some sort of expert that your Dr. Powell had flown in to help out with his work here."

"Powell's a nutcase," Timothy said. "Why the military would give him as much power as he has here is a mystery to me."

"Ah, come on, Timothy, fess up now," Mendez chided. "You must have been here a while by now. There's no way I'm buying that you don't know everything there is to know about whatever is going on here."

"I'm just a radar guy and comm officer," Timothy shrugged.

"My point exactly." Mendez finished his cigarette, lighting up another one.

"You really shouldn't be smoking in here," Timothy said, finally appearing to work up the backbone to call Mendez on breaking regulations. Mendez was a tough looking sort. He was only around five foot six but his body had the build of a professional fighter. A scar ran the length of his right cheek adding to his already gruff demeanor. Timothy, on the other hand, was your typical paper-pusher sort of officer and not a grunt. He was thin and mousy. Thick rimmed glass sat across the ridge of his nose and his hair was a stringy mess atop his head.

"You gonna report me?" Mendez leaned up against the console Timothy sat next to.

"No," Timothy shook his head. "Just making sure you knew."

"You and Stevens there are both too strung up. You guys really need to learn how to relax," Mendez grinned. "But we're all getting away from the issue at hand here. Is the lady do-able or not, Stevens?"

"Her name is Dr. Leia Carpenter," a voice boomed from behind them.

Stevens, Mendez, and Timothy all snapped to attention as they saw it belonged to Colonel Wilson.

"Sir!" they chorused as one.

The colonel walked over to Mendez and plucked the pilot's cigarette from his hand, stabbing it down into the mug that was being used an ashtray.

Mendez's earlier bravado was gone. His face grew pale, as Colonel Wilson looked him over.

"Timothy, give us a minute, would you." Colonel Wilson gestured for the radar tech to hustle it.

Timothy darted from the small room without looking back.

Colonel Wilson turned his gaze from Mendez to Stevens.

"The two of you may not be directly under my command here, but I warn you to tread carefully. The work happening here aboard Sonar Platform 1 is important to a lot people, myself included. I will not tolerate *anything* that could endanger it. Do I make myself clear?"

Stevens and Mendez nodded.

"Trust me, sir," Stevens glanced out the room's window, "as soon as the storm lets up, we'll be out of here as fast as we can."

"That's as it should be," Colonel Wilson approved. "None of us planned on the storm reaching the platform as fast as it has. It was not my intent to strand you here. That said, you gentlemen will not be allowed to venture into the platform's interior proper. This radar station has all the facilities you need and I will see to it that food and anything else you should need is delivered to you here."

"Thank you, sir," Stevens called after the colonel as Wilson turned and left the room.

After a moment, to make sure the colonel was gone, Mendez said, "Now that's one hardnosed son of a. . ."

"Language," Stevens interrupted him.

Mendez lit up a new smoke as he sat down to watch the storm raging outside. "You're too much a boy scout, Stevens, for your own good."

"Not really," Stevens argued. "I'm just a guy who wants to make it away from this place alive."

****

22

Captain Herc Locklin stood on the command deck of the U.S.S. Brighton. He was well used to life at sea but even so, he had to put effort into maintaining his stance. The storm's intensity continued to grow. The Brighton wasn't some massive carrier vessel. She was barely larger than a standard destroyer was. The waves splashing against her exterior hull along her waterline were beginning to play havoc with the functionality of her crew despite the best efforts of her engines to keep her as stationary as possible.

Herc's XO, Weaver, was a tall, rail thin man who had served with him for over a decade. Weaver was biting at the nail of his left pinky finger. Herc knew him well enough to know that meant trouble.

"You're worried about the storm," Herc commented.

Weaver stopped biting at his nail. "We've been through a lot worse over the years."

"That wasn't a real answer," Herc could see that Weaver didn't want to talk about whatever was really bothering him so he let the subject drop for the time being. "How are the Newton and Hall holding up?"

"As well as can be expected for ships their size. It would have been better on everyone if they had let us head to shore to ride this storm out," Weaver moved to look over the shoulder of the Brighton's helmsman. The helmsman nervously continued with whatever he was doing, trying to ignore the XO's presence.

"If this is as bad as it gets, we'll be fine." Herc moved to take a seat in his command chair. "According to the last reports, this storm system should be clear of the area by tomorrow at the latest."

"A lot can happen between now and then," Weaver frowned, opening up some. "I'm not as worried about us as much as I am about what's beneath the platform."

"Leave that to Wilson and his crew. That's his job, not ours."

"With respect, sir," Weaver said in his normal professional manner, "it'll be our job if that thing gets loose."

"It won't," Herc said firmly. "The riggings holding it are rated for a lot more than this storm is dishing out."

"So far, sir," Weaver agreed.

"Have a little faith, Paul." Herc straightened his uniform. "As you said, we have been through a lot worse than this."

"If it's all the same to you, sir," Weaver locked eyes with Herc, "I'll leave the faith part to you. Me, I am going to run a check on the CIWS and other systems to make sure we're ready if anything nastier than this storm does come our way."

****

Dr. David Powell hummed along with the music inside the elevator. Leia smirked that its sound system was blasting, "No More Mr. Nice Guy" at an ungodly volume.

"Picked the music for these lifts myself." Dave poked his chest with his thumb proudly.

"Could you turn it down some?" Leia shouted. "I think my ears are bleeding."

"What?" Dave raised a hand to his ear, mocking her. When she didn't smile, he moved to the elevator's controls and lowered the volume. "Sorry about that. Not an Alice Cooper fan I take it?"

"How far does this thing go down?" Leia asked.

"You'll see in a moment," Dave grinned at her.

The lift came to a stop and its doors slid apart, letting them out in a wide room with a transparent floor and matching walls. Leia panicked, diving back towards the lift's interior only to collide with Dave. He caught her, with a wicked smile spread over his lips. She realized her body was pressed up close to his, so she pulled away as quickly as she could.

"It's okay," Dave explained. "We're perfectly safe here. I keep Lightning so doped up, she isn't even conscious most of the time."

"Lightning…" Leia mumbled the word, remembering the name Dave had given to the Megalodon that he claimed to be keeping beneath Sonar Platform 1. She looked out through the thick, reinforced glass walls into the ocean beyond them.

The ocean close to Sonar Platform 1 was illuminated. A massive structure of riggings and metal poles held a creature that caused Leia's breath to catch in her throat. She stared at it in disbelief.

Lightning lolled about where she was restrained as the storm above stirred the water. Lightning was at least 100 feet long. The light of the riggings reflected keenly off the gray of her body. Leia guessed that she had to weigh over 300 tons. Despite being unconscious and a captive of the platform, Leia didn't doubt that Lightning was one of the most deadly killing machines on the planet.

Dave moved up beside her. "She's beautiful, isn't she?"

"I'm not sure that's the right word to describe her," Leia said before she could stop herself. "Isn't it dangerous keeping her like this?"

"She's barely aware of where she is most of the time. See these tubes running into her? They're pumping her full of enough sedatives to keep her as docile as a newborn child."

"Clearly, you don't know much about children."

"You know what I meant by the expression," Dave grunted.

If her words offended Dave, he didn't show it. He smiled and pointed at something in the water below where Lightning was held. "I don't blame you for not noticing them," he said, "Next to her, they're nothing…yet."

Leia's gaze followed Dave's gesture and she saw them. There were dozens of smaller sharks in the distance, restrained and held captive just like Lightning. They were only small in comparison to Lightning herself. Each of them was larger than a Great White. Their size was much close to the accepted size of natural Megalodons.

"They're my babies," Dave laughed. "Well, mine and Lightning's."

"What are they?" Leia muttered.

"I call them Hunters," Dave said proudly. "They're more scouts for Lightning than anything else."

"You're weaponizing them?" The disgust in Leia's voice came through loud and clear.

"That is what the military is paying me to do, yes,

but don't let that stop you from seeing the big picture, Dr. Carpenter. If I…we…can perfect my nano-tech's ability to interact perfectly with Lightning's brain, think about what a leap forward for humanity that would be. The medical applications alone are staggering."

"As are the destructive ones," Leia reminded him. "Do you really think the military will let you keep your tech after it's perfected?"

"All the non-military applications are my mine. It's in my contract and I hold the patent."

It was Leia's turn to laugh. "For someone as intelligent as you are, Dr. Powell, you are rather naive."

"I've worked numerous black ops like this one before and the military has always honored its word. You see, if they don't, they lose one of their best toy makers."

"I don't get it," Leia challenged Dave. "Those creatures of yours are impressive, I'll give you that but up against modern day naval vessels, are they really a threat?"

"Lightning is much more than she appears," Dave told her, "A great deal of work went into her. She was based on the recovered genetic material of a Megalodon, yes, but my team and I didn't stop there. Oh no. Her skeletal system is unique and hardened to withstand full on impacts, at her maximum speed, against enemy vessels. Her natural speed has been enhanced as well. Between her stealth attributes being a biologic, and the weapons she'll be carrying, she'll be a juggernaut of terror. Think of her as living, reusable weapons platform. And the Hunters carry internal explosive packs that can break the spine of the toughest battleships out there in addition to the armaments they'll be fitted with."

"Still. . ." Leia said.

"They aren't meant to engage larger surface vessels, Leia, though they can do with some limited degree of effectiveness."

Leia remained unconvinced.

"So many people claim that I fail to see the big picture. I think you are failing to do so now as well. Once my babies have been deployed, they'll also be our eyes and ears in the water. No surface, enemy vessel will see them as a true threat until it's far too late. We'll not only have exact positions and dispositions of any enemy force, but we'll have the means on site to deal with them as well. Beyond that, and this is the best part," Dave's look grew more and more feral, "think of the havoc and chaos these creatures, even without armaments, could cause to coastal regions and shipping lanes. Civilian vessels won't stand a chance against them. Entire economies could be crippled and populations panicked without *any* evidence pointing back to us."

Dave's manner changed as he waved his hand dismissively. "In truth, however, I don't care what the Navy uses them for Megalodons and sharks are among the most primal killers on this planet. If my nano-tech can override that nature, then it can override anything. What you're really looking at with my tech is the perfect means of mind and motor control for any living creature on Earth. *That* is why this project has received the funding and level of security that it has."

Leia let Dave's words sink in before responding. "What you're doing here is completely unethical. Give me one good reason why I should help you?"

"My dear, Dr. Carpenter," Dave's expression was deadly serious. "If you don't, someone else will."

****

Colonel Wilson finally made it to his quarters nearly three hours after arriving aboard Sonar Platform 1. He was exhausted. The trip in, and all that it entailed, had taken more of him than he wanted to admit. With an operation as large as this one, one's work was never really done.

His quarters were large by the platform's standard, equaling three normal size ones like the one that had been assigned to Dr. Carpenter. Only Dr. Powell's was larger. Wilson had his own personal bar, a workstation, his bunk, room for two extra chairs and a small conference table, in addition to the standard shower/toilet facilities.

He walked over to the bar, his eyes scanning for a bottle that fit his mood. They lingered for a moment on a bottle of red wine but then he bypassed it in favor of a bottle of Vodka. He lifted the bottle from where it sat on the bar's small shelf and unscrewed its top. Fetching a glass and some ice, he poured himself a glass as he picked up the remote that lay on the bar top and clicked on the room's stereo system. Geddy Lee's voice echoed off the room's wall belting out the lyrics to "The Twilight Zone."

With his drink in hand, Wilson took a seat at his

desk. He flipped open the laptop waiting for him there and entered the codes to override its security features. His fingers flew over its keys, calling up a file labeled "Ferret." The data it contained was even more classified than the Sonar Platform 1 project. Wilson had always suspected there was a spy aboard the platform but now he was sure. He had no hard proof yet, but his gut and years of experience told him it was true. It was his job to locate this individual before he or she could act. If word got out about the liberties Dr. Powell had with genetic research and cloning there would be hell to pay. Worse, if the world discovered the planned use for the good doctor's nano-tech, Wilson stood to lose a lot more than just his career.

When the bugs in Powell's nano-tech were dealt with, no one would be safe from it. A simple injection would give the military complete control over anyone they desired. Why go to war with another country when you could control its leaders or even perhaps someday its entire populace.

For all his efforts before leaving to bring Dr. Carpenter to the platform, he was no closer to discovering who the spy was nor could he enlist the aid of any of those under his command without endangering any chance he had of catching the spy he was after. Eventually, the spy would make a mistake and when that happened, Wilson swore he would be ready.

The presence of the two pilots worried him as well. Neither of them had the proper clearance to remain on the platform, but he couldn't simply order them to fly into the storm. That would be too blatant an act of murder. The trick was going to be making sure they stayed where they were in the helipad's radar tower. Keeping them confined there would not only reduce the risk of them stumbling onto something they had no business knowing, but also would allow his men to keep a direct watch over them.

Wilson sighed and drained his glass. He closed his laptop, frustrated and angry with himself at his inability to come up with a means of exposing the spy aboard Sonar Platform 1 before he or she acted.

Heading over to the bar, Wilson started to pour himself a second glass as alarm klaxons began to blare throughout the platform's interior.

****

Dr. Powell had walked Leia back to her quarters before finally letting her go. If she had been tired from the trip in, she was utterly exhausted now. She walked past her unpacked bags, flicking off the room's lights, and threw herself onto the room's small bunk. Leia rolled onto her back and stared up at the metal ceiling above her in the darkness. She knew she needed sleep but she couldn't get her mind to shut down. There were so many layers of cover to what Dr. Powell was doing here that she wasn't sure what the truth really was. All that she was completely sure of was that Sonar Platform 1 had nothing to do with the sonar experiments that it was on paper supposed to be conducting.

The image of Lightning, held there in the rigging beneath the platform, haunted her. Lightning was nothing less than horrific even sedated. Even a normal Megalodon would have been the top of any oceanic food chain but Lightning...she was in a class of her own. For man to take something already so monstrous and make it even more so was frightening. It chilled her to her bones. A creature like Lightning could swallow her whole. Alone, in the water, no one would stand a chance against something like her. She might even be able to bite through smaller ships, and larger civilian ones, she stood a good chance of overturning or at least damaging enough to leave them stranded and alone until she found a way to get at their crews. If the military perfected Powell's tech creatures like Lightning, they would be the ultimate weapons of terror in the world's oceans. Powell was also certainly right about the abject panic such creatures would cause if they struck a beach. The loss of civilian life... Leia forced herself to turn her mind from such violent and dark thoughts of churning red waters.

As terrifying as those thoughts were, the real possibilities of Powell's tech were even more troubling. If it could control creatures like Lightning, retasking those same nanos to control people wouldn't be that difficult. She couldn't help but wonder if Powell already created a version to be used on humans? Would he use it on her if she told the truth in her report? That seemed unlikely. Who in their right mind would believe half of the crap that was going on here?

Realizing she had unintentionally carried her data pad to the bed with her, she powered it up and began to review the files Powell had given her. The words on its screen swam around and she couldn't focus on what she was reading. Angry, she flung the data pad to the floor. It was built tough, so rationally, she was aware doing so wouldn't damage it. The act brought her a brief moment of release from the tension she felt.

Leia rolled over onto her side, curling up into a ball, and closed her eyes. She had no more begun to settle down finally, when the blaring noise of alarm klaxons sent her flying from her bed. She hit the floor hard, with the impact of her boots that she wore against the metal floor echoed in the confined space of her quarters.

Suddenly, the door to her quarters was jerked open. Melinda stood there, silhouetted by the bright lights of the corridor outside with her drawn sidearm in her hand.

"Come with me now!" Melinda barked at her.

"But. . ." Leia started to protest.

Melinda didn't give her the chance to finish her sentence. She grabbed Leia by her arm and tugged her along.

****

Dr. David Powell had been at work on a batch of nanobots in his private lab when the alarm sounded. He hopped up from his chair and raced to the vast array of monitors at his personal observation console. His gaze bounced from one screen to another. There was so much happening, too fast. Explosions were occurring all across Sonar Platform 1. Worse, they weren't confined to its surface structure. Dave watched in horror as the rigging that held his "children" collapsed. Lightning's massive body was released and it sunk downwards into the dark depths of the ocean. His Hunters came alive as they were released, the explosions waking them from their stupor. They darted away from the station and their former prisons so quickly that he caught little more than glimpses of their tail fins before they were gone.

"No!" he wailed. Tears welled up inside him. Something like what was happening should never have been possible. The military had promised that he and his work would be safe.

Dave ran full out across his lab to his private safe. Within it were a set of flash drives that contained the bulk of work alongside a tube of his nanobots. He input the safe's combination and jerked its door open, shoving the drives and tube into the pockets of his lab coat. With Sonar Platform 1 compromised, his first priority was to escape with his work. Dave had worked too long and too hard to watch it fall into the hands of anyone other than himself.

His second priority was to make sure there was no evidence left behind as he fled. Rushing back to his primary workstation, he logged into it and set in motion a virus of his own design to wipe the platform's systems and memory banks clean. He watched the virus begin its task before heading for the door that led into the platform's winding maze of corridors.

As he left his lab, he found Gregory sprinting towards him.

"Dr. Powell!" the platform's head of security yelled. "Thank God, you're alive!"

"No thanks to you," Dave spat instantly regretting his words.

Gregory skidded to a halt only inches away from where Dave stood.

"We can discuss that later, doctor," Gregory scowled. "Right now, we have to get you out of here and to somewhere safe."

And where would that be? Dave wondered. *We're in the middle of the ocean, with a storm raging around us, and my babies loose, uncontrolled, in the water!*

****

Mendez and Stevens watched the series of explosions ripping across the surface of the platform. A larger one sent an entire chunk of the platform sailing through the air to splash into the storm churned waters.

"Lord in heaven, have mercy on us," Mendez muttered.

"He might," Stevens shouted, "but those explosions won't!"

Stevens tackled Mendez, throwing the two of them to the deck, as an explosion detonated just outside the room they had been confined to. The wall next to them buckled inward from the blast. The window in it shattered, spraying shards of glass that flew like tiny missiles over them.

There was no sign of the radar tech, Timothy. He had never returned from Colonel Wilson ordering him out a few hours ago.

"What the devil is happening out there?" Mendez screamed. "It sounds like World War III!"

"How in the heck should I know?" Stevens growled, springing to his feet. "We need to get to the copter!"

He dragged Mendez up with him and the two of them headed together for the room's only door. It dangled on its frame, barely hanging on by a single, heavy hinge.

"What the frack? What the frack?" Mendez was babbling as Stevens shoved him along.

"Get it together, rookie," Stevens warned him. "Don't make me leave you here."

They bolted out of the platform's damaged radar station into the rain. It fell in waves so dense, it was hard to see more than a few feet ahead of where they were headed.

Steven's plan was simple. Get to their bird, fire up, and get the heck out of Dodge.

Rainwater ran down the flesh of Steven's face and neck, his clothes already soaked by the downpour. His brown hair was slicked to his scalp as he strained to see if their bird was still there and okay.

Both he and Mendez had to hang on tightly to the platform's railing to stay on their feet. The wind was so powerful that it was hard to breath.

"Even if she's there, we'll never make it to her!" Mendez shouted over the gale.

"We have to try!" Stevens shouted in response.

No sooner had the words left his lips than Stevens saw that his co-pilot was right. A bolt of lightning lit the dark skies and the rain seemed to part for a fleeting second. As it did, Stevens saw that their copter was gone. Well, mostly gone. One of the blasts had gutted it, leaving nothing more than a mangled mass of metal in its place.

"Frag!" Stevens' grip on the railing grew tighter.

"What is it?" Mendez demanded. "What did you see?"

"Our ride home is gone, man!"

"Hey! Is that a light over there?" Mendez cried, pointing to something close by to their position. "We've got to get out of this weather before it kills us!"

The two men painfully fought their way towards the light. The light was coming from inside the platform proper through a scattered access doorway. Stevens and Mendez dove through it. Their clothes and shoes made squelching sounds as they raced deeper down the corridor away from the rain and the raging storm.

****

The command deck of the USS Brighton was in chaos. Captain Herc gripped the arms of his chair so tightly that the flesh of his knuckles turned white. Despite the storm, he had heard the explosions rippling over Sonar Platform 1 even before the reports had begun to flood in. The Hall and Newton had confirmed those reports. Weaver, his XO, stood staring out the Brighton's forward window, his mouth hanging open in pure shock as other members of the bridge crew raced about around him.

"Weaver!" Herc snapped.

The XO turned to him still in a stupor of disbelief. "Sir?"

"Is the platform under attack?" Herc demanded.

"Negative sir," Weaver responded, shaking his head as if to clear it. "Whatever caused those explosions...it was aboard the platform."

"Sabotage," Herc gritted his teeth. "It has to be sabotage."

"Your orders, captain?" Weaver asked.

"Maintain our position. Order the Hall and the Newton to do the same. I don't want any of us getting too close to platform until we know...whatever that was is over."

Captain Herc got up from his chair. The storm was continuing to cause enough of a disturbance to make staying on his feet without effort difficult. "Hail the platform. We need to know if anyone is still alive over there."

"No response, sir!" his comm officer said. "That doesn't mean anything of course, sir. As bad as those explosions were, I'd be surprised if they even have power to their primary systems."

Herc glared at the comm officer. *Do you think I'm an idiot?* He thought, making a note to bring the woman up on charges later.

"I know that!" He yelled. "Just keep trying!"

"Uh, sir?" another bridge officer asked.

Herc spun on the young man. "What?"

"The biologics beneath the platform, sir. . ." the young officer stammered. "They're not there anymore."

Herc raced over to the sonar station where the officer sat. "What do you mean not there? Were they taken out in the blasts?"

The young officer was so intimidated by Herc's

presence and anger, his lips were moving but no words were coming out.

"Son," Herc said, "don't make me bash your face into that screen to get you to answer me."

"Between the storm and the debris from the explosions, it's impossible to say at this time if they were destroyed or freed," the young officer answered in one long, rapid-fire stream of words without pausing to take a breath.

"We should deploy some drones. Get a better idea of what's happened beneath the platform," Weaver suggested.

"Do it!" Herc ordered, taking a look out the Brighton's forward window at the mess the platform had become.

"Drones away!" Someone shouted.

"If those things are loose and uncontrolled. . ." Weaver started.

"Then God help us all," Herc finished for him.

****

Colonel Wilson woke up lying in the floor beside the bar in his quarters. The first thing he felt was pain. The glass he had been holding had shattered in his grasp as he had been flung from his feet. A large shard of it pierced his palm and there was a wet puddle of red around his hand.

He carefully hauled himself up into a sitting position and dug the shard out of his skin, tossing it aside. More red dripped into his field of vision. Wilson wiped at his forehead with the backside of his good hand. It came away covered in blood.

The last thing he remembered was the platform's

alarm klaxon howling to life. Whatever had followed had happened so fast that he hadn't even had the time to put his glass down, much less start for the door. He patted himself in search of more injuries to find none. His head hurt as if someone had taken a sledgehammer to it.

He got to his feet and grabbed a cloth napkin from atop the bar, using it as a makeshift bandage for his hand. Red seeped through it as he tied it as tightly as he could. *What the hell had happened?*

Stumbling out of his quarters into the corridor beyond, he realized the lighting was wrong. The lights in the corridor had shifted from their normal bright levels to an eerie tone of red. That meant the platform's primary power grid was down and everything was running on its backup generators.

Wilson drew the pistol he kept holstered on his belt and readied it. There was a *cha-chunk* sound as a round slid into its chamber. The gun made him feel better, if only somewhat so. His plan to wait for the spy aboard the platform and move to take them in custody then had failed. He wondered just how high a price he and the platform's crew paid for his failure.

Scanning his immediate surroundings for other survivors and seeing no one, dead or alive, Wilson opted to head for the platform's control room. At least there, he could get an idea of just how much damage had been done.

Cursing himself with every step, he picked up his pace, his stumbling gait becoming a more even jog towards the lift at the other end of the level from his quarters. He considered changing his course of action and checking on Powell first, but decided against it. If Gregory were alive, he would see to the good doctor. Wilson knew his responsibility lay with the project as a whole and for all he knew, he might very well be the last person left alive to salvage anything that could be saved.

****

Somewhere in the dark waters, far below the ruins of Sonar Platform 1, Lightning's massive form drifted. The sharp eyes of the world's deadliest predator came alive. The Megalodon rolled in the water, testing restraints that were no longer there. Lightning's giant mouth opened to show man sized razor teeth, five rows deep. Exhilaration coursed through her as she realized she was free. Her body flicked and propelled her both forwards and upwards. There were shapes moving about up there that called to her, and she was very hungry.

****

Melinda and Leia had been in one of the platform's lifts, headed for the surface structure when the explosions had detonated. Leia awoke to Melinda leaning over her.

"Dr. Carpenter?" Melinda was shaking her with one hand. "Dr. Carpenter, are you okay?"

Leia's eyes opened slowly as she came aware of her surroundings. The lift had stopped moving and its lighting had shifted to a pale shade of red. She ached all over from where she had been flung about the lift's interior. Her back hurt more than anything else did. The initial blast had thrown her into the lift's rear wall before bouncing her onto the floor.

"Just bruised and banged up," Leia told the security woman in a pained voice.

"Good," Melinda said and instantly got up, moving to the lift's doors. Leia saw that one of Melinda's arms was bound to the woman's chest by a makeshift sling of cloth torn from the uniform Melinda wore.

"Your arm," Leia said as she sat up.

"Broken," Melinda answered. Apparently noticing Leia's concern, she added, "I've had worse."

"I'm not a real medical doctor, but you should still let me take a look at it," Leia urged.

"No time," Melinda shook her head. "Our first priority has to be getting out of here."

"What's happened?" Leia asked as the tips of her fingers slipped up underneath her shirt to probe at her own injured back. She gritted her teeth, wishing she hadn't, as fresh waves of pain washed over her.

"Colonel Wilson has long suspected that there is an enemy agent aboard Sonar Platform 1. I'd wager that the agent has finally made their move."

"The lights?" Leia used the lift wall to help herself into an upright, standing position.

"They're on emergency power," Melinda explained. "Whatever happened appears to have knocked out the platform's main systems."

"You're saying that we're stuck here until help comes?"

"No," Melinda shot her a look. "I'm saying it's up to us to make our own way out."

Leia watched Melinda testing the lift's doors. "You're in no shape to be trying to open those by yourself. Here," she said, moving over to Melinda's side, "Let me help."

"It won't do any good," Melinda stepped away from the doors. "The blast that hit us bent them inside their frame. I doubt the two of us together could pry them apart now even if we had a crowbar to work with."

"So how do we get out then?"

Melinda pointed at the ceiling. There was a small hatch in the lift's top. "We need to get that open and climb up to the next level."

Leia stared at her in disbelief. "How are you going to climb with only one arm?"

"Let me worry about that after we get it open."

Noticing Melinda's pistol on the floor of the lift, Leia picked it up and handed it to the security woman.

"Thanks," Melinda took the weapon eagerly, cramming it into the holster on her hip. "I figure we're going to be needing this before all is said and done."

"And I think you're more shaken up than you think," Leia reached out and rested a hand on Melinda's shoulder. "Maybe we should wait for help."

"No, Dr. Carpenter. We can't. What if the help that shows up is whoever did this? We've got to keep moving, reach the surface, and get to one of the frigates."

Leia stood her ground. "How do you know it wasn't one of the frigates firing on the platform that did this?"

Melinda didn't answer her question. Instead, she motioned for Leia to move closer to her. "Here," she told her, "I'll give you a boost up to that hatch. You see if you can get it open."

Seeing that there was no reasoning with the security officer, Leia complied.

Melinda grunted as she helped Leia reach the hatch. To Leia's surprise, it opened easily.

"I got it!" Leia shouted.

"Crawl on up through it," Melinda ordered.

"What about you?"

"One thing at a time, blast it!"

Leia crawled on top of the lift and sat there in the darkness of the elevator shaft, looking down at Melinda. She braced herself as well as she could and leaned over the edge of the hatch's opening, lowering a hand inside the lift.

Melinda jumped up towards the opening, grabbing Leia, to pull herself the rest of the way up. Once there, the security officer slid a small flashlight free from her belt and flicked it on. The beam of light lit the shaft as Melinda waved it about, searching for something.

The two of them saw the ladder running up the side of the shaft at the same time.

"There!" Melinda pointed with the flashlight's beam. "That ladder will take us up to the next level. We should be able to force our way back into the platform's interior when we reach it."

"I suppose we should be thankful we don't have to climb up those," Leia motioned at the cables holding the lift in place.

"Come on!" Melinda growled. Leia couldn't tell if she was angry at the mess they were in or if the growl came from the level of pain Melinda had to be experiencing from her broken arm.

Leia carefully eased herself onto the ladder and started to climb. Melinda followed her at an impressive pace, considering her injured arm. Something creaked in the darkness above them. It had the sound of whining metal being stretched to the snapping point.

Below her, Melinda managed to get her flashlight placed in her teeth and raised her head up to shine the beam towards the noise. Leia heard Melinda mumbling a curse around the light she had just stuck in her mouth.

Leia looked up to see one of the doors above them hanging into the shaft. Whatever had rocked the entire platform had blown mostly out of its frame. It dangled over them, held where it was only by a tiny piece of metal that was in the process of breaking.

Neither of them could do anything as that tiny piece of metal gave way to the door's weight and the door came tumbling down the shaft towards them.

Leia closed her eyes, saying a prayer for divine mercy, as she pressed herself as flat against the ladder as she could. She felt a whoosh of moving air as the door past her. Below her, she heard Melinda scream and then the door struck the lift they had climbed out of.

The impact tore loose the cables keeping the lift in place. Door and lift alike dropped like a ton of bricks on down the shaft, vanishing from sight.

"Melinda!" Leia screamed.

"I... I'm still here," Melinda answered after an

eternity of silence ticked by. "The edge of that thing clipped my back so I suggest you keep moving. I don't know how much longer I can stay conscious and we need to get up to that doorway and through it."

Leia sped on up the ladder like a panicked squirrel. She threw herself through the open door when she reached it and rolled around to look down for Melinda, but the security officer was already at the doorway, staring her in the face.

"Out of my way!" Melinda warned, showing her teeth.

Leia scurried from her path as Melinda hauled herself into the corridor. The two of them sat side by side, exhausted, their breath coming in ragged gasps.

"That was too close," Melinda said and then slid over sideways onto the corridor floor.

"Melinda," Leia cried, rushing to grab her.

Her hands came away soaked in blood. Melinda's back was a mess. The edge of the falling door had sliced a jagged wound down the length of her back. Leia could tell at a glance, it was bad. Very bad.

Instinctively, Leia's hand shot to her where her data pad normally rested on her hip only to discover it wasn't there. She had hoped to call up a map of the platform and somehow get Melinda to the closest aid station or sickbay, but no such luck on that front. Without her pad to guide her, she was lost. Leia had no idea where she had lost her pad. She couldn't even remember if she had grabbed it when Melinda showed up at her quarters. Still, she had to do something.

Close by, there was a data station on the wall in

the corridor. Leia leaped up and raced to it only to find that with the platform's main power offline, it was too. She slammed a fist into its screen in her fury. The blow did not damage the data station, but Leia's knuckles came away from the impact bruised and scuffed. She slung her hand about in the air trying to shake off the pain.

"Idiot," she heard Melinda croak weakly from where she lay.

"Oh, thank God!" Leia exclaimed. "I thought I had lost you."

"No such luck yet," Melinda started to laugh but her face twisted with pain.

"Get me on my feet," Melinda demanded, "There's an aid station on this level, a few doors down."

****

"That…that's messed up," Dave commented as he and Gregory jogged past the body of one of the platform's crew that had been almost severed in half by shrapnel from an imploding wall. The man lay in the floor of the corridor, his upper half several feet from his lower one. The two pieces were connected solely by a long strand of blue and purple intestines. The rest of the man's intestines coiled around the ends of his two halves like bloated snakes. The man's mouth was open as if in a scream and drips of blood dropped from it into the small pool staining the floor beneath his head.

"He died fast." Gregory continued dragging Dave along, not letting him stop to stare at the mess. "I'm sure that's better than what the crew got out of whatever happened here."

"Stop!" Dave pleaded. "I'm gonna throw up."

Gregory skidded to a halt and let go of the good doctor.

Dave hunched over and vomited up the contents of his stomach, violently, not far from where the dead lay. Dry heaves continued shaking him long after his stomach was empty.

"You good?" Gregory barked.

Dave wiped his mouth clean with the backside of his hand. "No, I'm not."

"Too bad," Gregory jerked Dave up. "We have to keep moving anyway."

"Wait!" Dave cried, slapping Gregory's gripping hand off him. "Do you hear that?"

Gregory snarled at Dave as he stopped to listen.

The sound was that of rapid footsteps. Someone was running towards their position from one of the adjoining corridors.

Gregory motioned for Dave to keep quiet, drew the pistol holstered on his belt and got ready to meet them. Both men waited silently to see who rounded the corner ahead of them.

"Colonel Wilson!" Dave yelled as the man came into view.

Wilson skidded to a halt. "Gregory, thank God. . ." the colonel started but never got the chance to finish his sentence. Gregory's pistol barked three times in rapid succession. The first round caught Wilson in his left shoulder, almost spinning him around. With an impressive effort, Wilson managed to not only fight to hold his body facing Gregory, but draw his own pistol as well. Gregory's second shot knocked it from his grasp as it hammered into Wilson's stomach, causing the colonel to fold up, doubling over towards the floor. Gregory's third shot missed, whizzing through the air where the colonel's head had been a fraction of a second before.

Dave was paralyzed by fear, not having the slightest idea why the two men would be shooting at each other…but they were.

Wilson thudded to the floor, rolling, as Gregory took a fourth shot at him. The round sparked off the metal of the corridor's wall near where Wilson had been. The colonel was already on his feet though, his gun aimed at Gregory. The colonel managed a single wild shot before Gregory's fifth one took him out. It struck Wilson dead on in the throat. Blood sprayed into the air as Wilson's head was knocked back from the bullet. His body reeled and finally hit the floor again to move no more.

"What in the Hades did you do that for?" Dave shrieked.

Gregory spun on him, the butt of the security officer's pistol slamming into the side of his jaw. Dave staggered to lean up against the corridor's wall, spitting teeth and blood. When he looked at Gregory again, his gaze was filled with a burning anger.

"It was you," Dave groaned, holding his nearly broken jaw with the fingers of his left hand. "You did this."

"We can do this easy way or the hard way, Dr. Powell. It's up to you," Gregory informed him. "But my employer has asked me to bring you in alive. You are a lot more valuable than those samples you're

49

carrying. Don't think for a second I won't settle for them though. If you make me, I'll be just as glad to leave your body right there next to the colonel's."

"Why?" Dave asked, wiping blood from his busted lip.

Gregory snorted. "Why does anyone do anything, doctor? The money of course."

"I'll pay you triple the amount you're getting if you just let me walk out of here," Dave offered, hoping Gregory would go for it.

"You're rich, doctor, but not that rich." Gregory extended an open hand towards him. "Now give me the samples you're carrying and let's keep moving before someone else comes along."

Dave met Gregory's eyes and then moved his gaze to the gun being pointed at him. He wasn't a fighter, never had been. If Gregory wanted him dead, there was nothing to stop him. With a heavy sigh, he dug the flash drives and tube of nanos from his pockets, placing them into Gregory's waiting palm.

"Good boy," Gregory grinned. "Now if you would be so kind. . ."

Gregory waved the barrel of his pistol, indicating that he wanted Dave to walk in front of him.

"You'll never get away with this," Dave said as moved past Gregory and started along the corridor.

"Spare me the clichés, doctor," Gregory said, "because I already have."

****

Captain Derek Spraker of the USS Hall wasn't in the mood to take any crap. He had job to do and he was dang well going to see it done.

"I said to bring us alongside the platform," Spraker repeated.

"But sir. . ." Daniel, the Hall's helm officer protested again. "The platform is still on fire and with the storm, maintaining any sort of safe position to the platform will be impossible."

"I didn't ask your opinion, Lieutenant. I gave you an order and I want to see it carried out. Now."

"Yes sir." Daniel leaned forward over the Hall's helm and began the process of bringing the frigate up as close to the platform as he could.

"Sir, we have an unknown, subsurface contact CBDR and it's coming up fast!"

What the devil? Spraker wondered. *That doesn't make any sense!*

The Hall was an old class, Cyclone style frigate. She had been retrofitted though for the Sonar Platform 1's mission directive. Instead of her normal complement of surface to air missiles, she now carried torpedo launchers as well as an allotment of depth charges.

"The unknown contact will make impact us in less than a minute, sir!"

Spraker cursed himself for his hesitation. "Take the contact with guns and blow it to hell!" he ordered.

"Torpedoes away!" the gunnery officer informed him. "Impact in three. . .two. . .one. . ."

The explosions of the detonating warheads of the torpedoes beneath the Hall caused the ship to buck upwards on the already storm churned waters. Spraker lost his footing on the deck. He plunged into Daniel where the younger officer sat at the helm, knocking Daniel from his seat. The two of them ended up as a rolling mass of flailing limbs.

Spraker threw Daniel to the side, getting the young man off him and leapt to his feet.

"Report!" he barked.

"The subsurface contact appears to have broken up, sir! It...*they*... " the sonar tech corrected himself, "...are veering away for us!"

"We hit it, didn't we?" Spraker fumed, "What do you mean it's veering away?"

"I said *they* sir." The sonar tech was struggling to keep his voice level and calm. "The original contact appears not to have been a solid mass but rather a cluster of some kind that dispersed as our torpedoes detonated."

"Powell's sharks," Spraker muttered as understanding dawned on him.

"That would be my guess as well, Captain," the sonar tech agreed.

"Do we know if any of them were armed when the platform was hit? Are we just facing animals here or armed to the teeth ship killers?"

"Negative, sir. According to the last report we got from Group Captain Locklin, Colonel Wilson had confirmed that all the biologics were sedated and inactive."

Spraker mulled that over as the sonar tech spoke up again. "The contacts appear to be keeping below the surface and are proceeding at presumed maximum speed away from us and the platform."

"Lock guns onto them anyway," Spraker ordered. "I want to know for sure those things aren't going to be a problem for us."

"Yes sir!" The gunnery officer nodded and went about carrying out the order.

****

"The Hall reports that they have been unable to close in to Sonar Platform 1 and begin rescue operations," Weaver informed Captain Herc Locklin aboard the USS Brighton.

"Why the Hades not?" Herc asked, leaning forward in his command chair.

"They were engaged by a group of biologics, sir," Weaver reported. "Captain Spraker says the biologics are not a threat sir and he has begun eliminating them to clear the area for another vessel to make the rescue attempt you ordered."

Herc frowned as Weaver stared at him. "Maintain our position here and order the Newton to move up to the platform. If there's anyone left alive over there, we need to get some help to them as quickly as possible now that the threat of more explosions has decreased."

Twisting about in his chair to look at his comm officer, Herc asked, "Any luck getting through to the personnel aboard the platform?"

"No sir," the officer answered. "I've been continuing to establish contact, as you ordered, since the explosions stopped."

"Keep at it," Herc said as he watched Weaver walked over towards his command chair.

"Captain Spraker didn't say which biologics he had engaged," Weaver pointed out.

"Yeah, I noticed that too," Herc agreed. "At the

time of the explosions, those sharks below the station were supposed to be drugged up and tucked in all nice and snug like."

Weaver nodded. "If that was truly the case, then only the good doctor's pride and joy would a threat to us. Spraker may be wasting a lot of time and ammo for nothing. Are you going to call him back?"

Herc shook his head. "Spraker's more of a help to us chasing down those rogue sharks than he would be here and you know it. The man's never been able handle any kind of stress well. If it weren't for the flaming batch of bleeding heart liberals in office now, there's not a chance in hell that he'd gotten the command that he has."

Weaver grinned at Herc's assessment of Spraker but didn't argue with it. Instead, he asked, "What about Lightning herself? How do we deal with her if she shows up?"

"I'm hoping she won't," Herc admitted. "We've got enough to deal with already."

****

"Was that gunfire?" Mendez panicked. "Tell me that wasn't gunfire we just heard."

"Sure sounded like it."

Stevens and Mendez stood in what once must have been the Sonar Platform 1's main mess hall. The place was little more than wreckage, which was filled with the bodies of several of the platform crew. One particularly messy corpse lay only a few feet from them next to the shattered remnants of a table. The woman must have been sitting right next to where the bomb that took out the mess had been planted. The top half of her body was twisted around towards them above the stumps that her legs were once attached to. Most of the flesh of her chest was gone. Stevens could see the broken bones of her ribs clearly through the pulped mass of tissue hanging from them. The upper right side of the woman's head was gone as well. Pieces of brain matter had been splashed onto the floor around her.

"Heck of a way to die," Stevens said, sure he looked as green as he felt and trying not to throw up in front of Mendez. His co-pilot was barely holding it together as things were.

"Forget about her!" Mendez grabbed him. "Was that freaking gunfire? And if so, what the heck are they shooting at?"

Stevens fought free of Mendez's white knuckled grip on him, shoving Mendez away before he answered, "You know as much as I do, man! I told you this black op stuff had a way of getting you killed. Do you believe me now?"

Mendez looked as if he wanted to punch him, but managed to hold himself in check at the last possible second.

"Sorry," Stevens held up his hands in a gesture of peace. "Just give me a second to think, okay?"

"That gunfire was pretty close, bro," Mendez protested. "We may not have a second."

"Calm down," Stevens told him. "There's no way whoever is out there could possibly know we're in here. Just keep quiet and we should be fine."

Mendez didn't appear convinced but he kept his mouth shut all the same.

"Now help me dig through these bodies," Stevens whispered.

"What for?" Mendez went pale at the thought.

"If whoever is out there is hostile, then we're going to need some firepower of our own before we run into them." Stevens shuddered as his hands closed on the remains of a woman and shifted her corpse about to see if she was wearing a holster. "Somebody here might have had a gun on them when they died and if they did, we *need* it."

Three minutes later, Stevens and Mendez were covered in gore. Red smeared their still rain soaked uniforms but they had lucked out. Amid the corpses had been two bodies with sidearms holstered to them and there was a loose M-16 lying under a piece of metal debris.

Stevens gave Mendez one of the pistols, keeping the other pistol and the rifle for himself. He tucked the pistol carefully under his belt and held the M-16 at waist level after making sure it was loaded and its safety was disengaged. Stevens hoped he wouldn't really have to use the weapon but having it was better than not having it given the circumstances.

Having a weapon in his hands appeared to calm Mendez down a good bit too. "I haven't heard any more shots, have you?"

"No." Stevens kept a watchful eye on the mess hall's doorway just in case he was wrong and whoever had fired the shots they had heard appeared at it.

"Think we should go check out the ones we heard?"

"What else are we gonna do?" Stevens shrugged.

"I don't think I can handle staying in here much longer."

"Truth," Mendez agreed. "You first."

Stevens headed out of the mess hall with Mendez following him.

****

Leia had helped Melinda onto the sickbay bed and left her there as she searched the room for the tools she would need to patch the security officer up. She wasn't a real doctor but she knew enough about basic biology to fake it well enough to count.

Melinda was fading in and out of consciousness. Her groans were coming farther and farther apart from one another. Leia knew that wasn't a good sign. Neither was the amount of red that stained the bedsheets under where Melinda lay.

Being careful of Melinda's broken arm, Leia rolled her over. She was glad to see the wound wasn't as bad as she thought it was. Despite its looks, a good portion of its bleeding had already stopped. Leia stitched up the wound and got it bandaged as fast as she could. Lifting Melinda to get the bandages around her was not an easy task. When it was done, Leia hooked up an IV to keep Melinda hydrated and hopefully it would stimulate the woman's own blood production. Those things done, Leia took a good, long look at Melinda's arm, studying the fracture there. It was going to have to be dealt with too.

As Leia snapped the bone roughly back into place, Melinda came awake with a scream. Her good hand shot out, fingers closing around Leia's neck. Leia's hands locked around the one that held her as she fought to breathe. Melinda's grip was like a vice around her throat. The woman was too strong to break free from. Leia changed tactics and punched Melinda in the temple with all the force she could muster. The security woman reeled but her hold on Leia remained firm another few seconds as Melinda became aware of what she was doing and whom she was doing it to. Only then did Melinda let Leia go.

Leia flew backwards, colliding with a table of medical tools, as she sucked in huge gasps of air, trying to refill her lungs. "What the hell?" Leia shouted as soon as she got enough oxygen inside her to speak.

Melinda had slumped back onto the bed. "Instinct," she croaked. "Sorry."

"Some thanks I get for saving your lousy butt!" Leia found herself giggling.

"You owed me a few," Melinda tried to smile but it didn't truly form and resembled something more akin to a playful snarl.

"I'll have to remember we're keeping count," Leia half sat, half collapsed into the chair by the bed Melinda lay on. It was all she could do to keep her own eyes open. The adrenaline of their panicked flight through the platform had long abated. She could only wonder at the level of strength and determination that Melinda had to have in order to even be conscious at all given her wounds. Leia's fingers unconsciously rubbed at the bruises on her throat where the security woman had grabbed her.

"We need to keep moving," Melinda tried to get up and failed.

"You stay right where you are," Leia leaned forward to place a hand on Melinda, holding the security woman down, "I don't think you're quite ready for that yet."

"It's not safe here."

"Nothing we can do about that now. Rest a while. Somebody has to have sent for help by now."

"Don't count on it," Melinda told her and then finally did give in to the toll the last few hours had taken on her. She lay unconscious, leaving Leia alone, watching over her.

****

Captain Derek Spraker was greatly enjoying himself. This was the most action the Hall had seen in two weeks and this time it was real, not just some test that Dr. Powell had them running against his creatures.

"Batteries released!" The Hall's gunnery officer said loudly.

Half a minute ticked by before the sonar tech added, "Contact! That's the last of them, sir!"

Spraker allowed himself a smile. He didn't give a crap how much Powell had invested in the sharks he'd just blown to bits. Given the current circumstances with the attack on Sonar Platform 1, there wasn't a court martial board in the world that could find him guilty of any misconduct. Those sharks were a threat to any survivors left aboard the platform and a threat to the efforts being made to rescue them as well.

The Hall's bridge crew was cheering and celebrating around him. Sure, it wasn't exactly heroic to go up against a group of sharks in a modern day naval vessel, but it was one heck of a stress reliever.

"Good work, people," Spraker told his crew.

"Sir, the Newton has just radioed that they have docked with Sonar Platform 1 and rescue operations are underway," The Hall's comm officer shouted over the continued celebrating.

Spraker smiled. *It's shaping up to be a good day after all.*

"Captain!" the sonar tech yelled at him. "We have another contact, CBDR!"

"Battle stations!" Spraker shouted at the top of his lungs, reining in the good spirits of his bridge crew.

The celebration ended as quickly as it had begun.

"I thought you said that was the last of them?" Spraker challenged his sonar tech.

"It was sir," the tech said. "This is a new subsurface contact, not one that we missed."

"Time to contact?" Spraker asked.

Before the tech could answer, something massive slammed into the bottom of the USS Hall. The Hall lurched up out of the waves, nearly overturning, before splashing back down.

"Damage report!" Spraker snapped.

"Hull integrity has been compromised. We're taking on water!"

"What the Hades hit us?" Spraker demanded.

"Unknown," the sonar tech answered him, leaning intently over his console. "Whatever it was is moving at close to 60 knots! It's circling around to make another run at us!"

"Lightning," Spraker breathed, going pale.

Powell's prize monster.   That was the only explanation.

"Take contact with guns!" Spraker ordered.

"The contact is too close, sir!" The gunnery officer exclaimed, panicked. "If we fire, we'll put ourselves at risk!"

There was no time for Spraker to order anything else. He stood up from his command chair and looked out the forward observation window to see a giant fin sticking out of the waves on a direct course for the Hall. His brain barely had time to process what he saw before the Megalodon crashed into the Hall once more. The impact sent Spraker flying across the bridge. Systems were shorting out all around him. Consoles and workstations exploded into flames. Members of his crew were screaming; some of them on fire themselves.

The force of Lightning's impossibly large body slamming into the Hall's side caved in her hull where the giant creature impacted it. The Hall did roll over this time. Water came rushing onto the bridge, sweeping up the members of her crew caught in its path.

Spraker floated above the floor of the bridge as the Hall sank deeper into the raging water. He knew he was dead. Even if he made it clear of the ship, he'd stand no chance in the open waves against that *thing* outside. Refusing to surrender without a fight, he swam towards the Hall's now shattered forward window. He made it less than a foot before something checked his movement, dragging him to a halt. He glanced back to see his sonar tech clinging desperately to him. The man's eyes were wide and his mouth open. There were no bubbles escaping it though. The tech was already dead and it must have latched onto him as his final act. A piece of the console he'd been leaning over had wedged itself into the man's skull as it had exploded. Spraker struggled to free himself but couldn't. Finally, his own breath escaped his lungs and salt water replaced it as his body thrashed about in its death throes.

****

"We've lost contact with the Hall," Weaver informed Herc.

Their ship, the Brighton, was holding back, still a good distance from Sonar Platform 1. Herc inwardly cursed Spraker for being a fool. *Couldn't the man even take out a few sharks without screwing it up somehow?*

"I thought you just said the Hall had reported in that the last of the sharks had been eliminated?"

"Apparently not all of them, sir." Weaver frowned.

"Sir," the Brighton's sonar/radar tech cut in, "the Hall is gone."

"Define gone?" Herc stared at the man.

"She's been capsized, sir," the tech answered, "and it is sinking fast."

"Dear God, help us," Herc muttered. "It's Lightning. It has to be."

"Hoping that she was killed by the attack on the station or that she would simply leave the area if those explosions freed her was perhaps a tad too much in terms of wishful thinking," Weaver sighed.

"Sound battle stations!" Herc ordered. "And warn

the Newton!"

Alarm klaxons blared aboard the Brighton as its crew rushed to their stations.

"If anything, and I mean *anything,* comes towards us in the water, I want it blown to hell!"

Herc thought about the Newton. She was sitting completely exposed, docked with Sonar Platform 1. If that big freaking killing machine Powell created came at them. . .

"Bring us closer to the platform," Herc ordered. "We need to shield the Newton if that thing decides to come back this way."

"Is that wise?" Weaver cautioned.

"What other choice do we have?" Herc said. "We can't just leave them there."

"Understood," Weaver nodded and darted across the bridge to make sure Herc's orders were being carried out.

****

Gregory opened the door and shoved Dr. David Powell through it into the wind and rain ahead of him. The doctor had been silent most of the way to the platform's surface. Gregory had hoped that the Newton would be the ship tasked with rescuing the platform's personnel. He had contacts aboard it who would make his escape a manageable thing. Either of the other two ships would have presented a problem. Dragging Powell onto the Hall or worse, the Brighton, at gunpoint would have been a much more difficult thing to explain. Hope swelled within him as he saw two men, who wore the insignia of the Newton, running towards them.

Grabbing Dave, he jerked the doctor close to him. "Keep it cool, doc, and I won't have to put a bullet in your back."

Gregory released Dave and waved his arms in the air at the men rushing to rescue them. "Over here! I've got Dr. Powell with me!"

The wind was horrible, but overall, the storm had died down some. The clouds remained dark and the rain continued to fall in a full out downpour but it was possible to stand on the platform's deck without being blown off it.

The two men from the Newton met Gregory and Dave, helping them to where the ship was docked.

"What happened here?" One of the men asked.

"Sabotage," Gregory answered, shoving Dave into the waiting arms of the two men from the Newton. "The good doc here decided the powers that be weren't paying him enough. He took out the platform with IEDs he was able to place around its structure without being questioned."

The two men stared at Dave as if he were a demon that had crawled up from the depths of hell. One of them slammed Dave up against a wall and produced a pair of handcuffs. He slapped them onto Dave as the doctor cried out. The man's roughness in applying the cuffs had nearly dislocated one of his shoulders.

"You've got the wrong man!" Dave wailed. "He's behind all this, not me!"

The man who cuffed him slammed Dave into the wall again. Dave felt his breath leave his lungs. As he gasped for air, the man gave him an *I'm not going to put up with your crap* look. Seeing there was no point in trying to get the men to see reason, he gave up, his shoulders slumping in defeat.

Gregory flashed his teeth at Dave in a mocking smile.

"Are there any other survivors?" one of the men from the Newton asked Gregory.

Gregory craned his neck around and took a long look at the exit from where he and the doctor had emerged.

"Sir?" the man prompted him again. "Did you hear me? Are there any more survivor aboard this platform?"

Gregory checked his watch and then shook his head. "No, we're it."

"Come on then," the man said. "This little freak's monster is loose! We have to get out here while we can!"

****

Leia took the glass of water away from Melinda's lips after the security woman had gotten a good drink from it.

"Thanks," Melinda grunted.

Putting the glass aside, Leia leaned over Melinda checking the splint she had placed on her arm.

"You feel ready to move yet?" Leia asked.

"What time is it?" Melinda asked.

Leia was taken by surprise at the strange question. "I don't know. I don't have a watch, and if you haven't noticed, the power is out," Leia finished with a sarcastic grin.

"My cell is in my left pants pocket," Melinda said, "Can you get it out?"

Gingerly, Leia retrieved the cell and powered it on. As she suspected, it had no signal or Melinda would've tried to use it before now. Glancing at the time on its display, Leia said, "It's almost 7 PM."

"How close?" Melinda's voice had an edge of desperation to it.

"Five 'til," Leia answered, still not understanding why Melinda was suddenly so obsessed with the time.

"I'm sorry," Melinda reached for Leia hand. Leia met her halfway, taking her hand in her own.

"You don't need to be sorry," Leia laughed, "We're not dead yet. Help's coming. You'll see."

"No, it's not," Melinda said firmly. "And if it is, they'll just die with us."

"I don't understand."

"My job was to get you out of here, Dr. Carpenter, and I failed. The people paying me wanted you as much as they wanted Dr. Powell and samples of his work."

'What?" The world seemed to spin around Leia as she began to understand what Melinda was admitting to.

"Powell's nano-tech is priceless," Melinda clenched her teeth, trying to raise up some from the bed.

"Your back," Leia let go of Melinda's hand. "Let me get you some more pain meds."

"No," Melinda ordered. "Gregory and I were behind it all. Don't you get it? We're the ones who set the bombs that tore this place apart. It was all part of Gregory's plan. He and I were going to use the money we were getting to disappear and start over. My part of his plan was to round you up and get you aboard the Newton while he got Powell. Once the two of you were delivered to that ship, we would have been set for life."

Leia got up and stood over Melinda. "You...you did all this?"

Melinda nodded.

"Why are you telling me this now?" Leia demanded to know.

"Because in another minute or two, it won't matter," Melinda sighed. "You see, we couldn't take a chance on leaving any of Powell's work behind for someone else to find and build on. Not to mention, Gregory is a fan of tying up loose ends."

"No witnesses," Leia whispered.

"Exactly," Melinda went on. "We set one final bomb; one powerful enough to take out the entire platform."

Melinda was still talking as Leia flew out the sickbay's door and vanished from her sight. Laughing through the pain that she felt, Melinda paused, catching her breath, and then said, "You go, girl. It won't do you any good though. We're both dead."

****

Stevens and Mendez crept along the corridor with Stevens in the lead. Stevens held the M-16 he carried at the ready. There hadn't been anymore gunshots in some time. Both men were pressed to their limits and on edge. Their path in investigating the earlier shots had taken them deeper and deeper into the platform's structure.

They rounded a corner and came across the body of a man lying on the floor. They had seen many corpses during their passage through the platform's interior, but this one had to be the one they were looking for. Stevens could see the jagged exit wound of a high caliber round on the backside of the man's soldier. He squatted beside the body and rolled it over.

Colonel Wilson's head lolled back as Stevens moved him, exposing the grizzly carnage of where a bullet had shredded his throat. Stevens leapt to his feet, backing away from the colonel's body.

"Is that…?" Mendez asked.

"Yep," Stevens confirmed. "That's Colonel Wilson. Looks like somebody shot him up pretty good too."

"What the hell?" Mendez sputtered. ""I thought he was in command here."

"I imagine he did too," Stevens shrugged and then reached down to pick up the pistol that rested on the floor near the colonel's body. "Right up until the moment he rounded that corner," Stevens gestured at the one they had just rounded themselves.

"Holy crap," Mendez scanned the area around them as if he were expecting the colonel's killer to pop out and take a shot at them too.

"Relax," Stevens said, "whoever did has to be long gone by now."

"How can you know that?"

"Think about it, man," Stevens explained. "If you filled the CO of this place with bullets, would you hang around to see who showed up to find his body?"

The sound of a woman's scream ripped Steven and Mendez's attention to the far end of the corridor they stood in.   The two of them watched in shock as Dr. Carpenter came tearing towards them.

Mendez jerked up his pistol, his reflexes overriding his rational mind.   Stevens brought his hand down onto to Mendez's arm, saving Dr. Carpenter's life as his co-pilot squeezed the trigger. The bullet sparked off the metal floor, ricocheting around the corridor.

Carpenter stopped in her tracks, skidding to a halt. She flung her hands above her head and screamed, "Don't shoot!   Please don't shoot!"

Stevens gave Mendez a shove and stern look. Mendez let his weapon clatter to land at his feet, as Stevens made sure the barrel of his M-16 was pointed downwards and away from the doctor.

"Dr. Carpenter?" Stevens asked.   "Is that really you?"

Recognition dawned in the woman's eyes. "You're the pilot that flew me here!   Stevens!"

"Yes, ma'am." Stevens moved and took her in his arms, seeing that she was so upset that she was shaking.   She pushed away from him with an expression of utter terror on her face.

"There's another bomb," she told them.   "It's set to detonate in. . ."

Dr. Leia Carpenter never finished her sentence.   A thunderous blast shook the corridor and in its wake, before any of them could so much as move, a wall of fire swept over the three of them.   The heat of the fire melted their flesh from their bones, cooking them alive where they stood.

****

Gregory had just been led onto the command deck of the USS Newton when the shock waves from the explosion engulfing the whole of Sonar Platform 1 struck. The Newton was thrown sideways in the water. Gregory lost his footing and met the deck of the ship face first. He heard the crunch of bone as his jaw broke and several of his teeth shattered from the impact. He could hear the ship's XO, Geoff, shouting orders and demanding a damage report.

The Newton's captain lay a few feet from Gregory. A thick shard of glass from the ship's forward observation window protruded from his right eye. Red seeped out around the embedded glass. Gregory could see it had hit the captain from behind and cut its way cleanly through his skull.

Scrambling to his feet, Gregory spat broken pieces of his teeth onto the deck. They landed with wet splashing noise, the spit around them thick with blood. Gregory hands patted over his chest and sides searching for more injuries. Other than his jaw, he seemed okay. If you could call the amount of pain he was in okay anyway. He tried to speak, ask the XO how badly the Newton had been damaged, but all his efforts produced were more pain and strands of red drool that leaked from his messed up mouth.

"We've got incoming!" Someone shouted. "It's the damn Megalodon!"

Gregory staggered to stand behind the ship's empty command chair, watching the panic and chaos around him. There were small fires burning in several places on the bridge. He saw the bodies of two other dead crewmen, one sitting limply at the ship's blown out comm station and the other near the bridge's only exit. He recognized the second as the officer who had seen him to the bridge.

"Guns," the XO wailed. "Lock onto that monster and let it know it's not the only thing in the water that has teeth!"

Strangely, as Gregory imagined hearing the torpedoes launching from the Newton's subsurface tubes, he thought of Melinda. Leaving her to die on the platform had never been part of the plan. He felt a pang of guilt sting him. Melinda was one hot lady, but he had never loved her, not really. Gregory admitted to himself that were certain aspects of having her in his life he was going to miss though. With the amount of cash he was being paid for this gig though, he assured himself, she would be replaced easily enough. The comfort that thought brought him didn't last long.

"What do you mean you missed the thing?" The XO howled, racing towards the ship's gunnery officer as if he was going to beat the man to a pulp at his station with his bare hands.

"Contact is turning!" the Newton's sonar tech shouted. "It's coming around at us again."

"Evasive maneuvers!" The XO yelled but it was too late and the Newton was too heavily damaged. The Newton's engines whined, the helmsman pouring on all the power he had at his disposal, but there was no escaping the enraged Megalodon.

Gregory peered out through the shattered forward

window and saw the massive thing leap out of the water. It was like watching some primordial god raising from the depths. It splashed down into the waves vanishing from Gregory's line of sight as fast as it had appeared. The impact of the Megalodon striking the Newton was the end. As the ship's hull bent inward, the live ammo being reloaded into its firing tubes was jarred in just the *wrong* way. Gregory's world went white as the Newton blossomed into a blazing fireball on the ocean's surface.

****

First Sonar Platform 1 went up liking a detonating nuke. The Newton followed her in a matter of minutes. Herc and Weaver had no idea what had happened on board the platform, but it was clear what destroyed the Newton. Herc could see the giant, gray fin speeding away from the Newton's blazing wreckage. Lightning had made her second kill of the night.

"There' no way anyone could have survived that," Herc gestured at the flaming ruins of Sonar Platform 1.

"No argument here, sir," Weaver agreed. "I would venture that our job here is done."

"That doesn't mean it's over," Herc said. "That Megalodon out there needs to be dealt with."

Weaver looked at him as if he were insane.

"I didn't mean by us," Herc slapped Weaver on the shoulder. "I'm not an idiot. Could we even take her if we tried?"

"Tactical assessment, sir?" Weaver asked. "Honestly, I don't know. She's big, she's fast, and worst of all, she's smart. She knows us and our capabilities to an extent as well from our time here stationed at Sonar Platform 1 and the exercises Dr. Powell had us run with her."

"That wasn't an answer," Herc growled, the frustration he was feeling slipping through into the tone of his voice.

"No, sir, it wasn't. The Newton gave her a good fight. It's likely that she didn't come away from it unscathed, given how the Newton went up. If she was injured, that may slow her down and tip the odds of us at least getting out of here alive in our favor."

"So you don't think we can take her?"

"Not on our own," Weaver answered. "Not without a miracle anyway. If we had a *real* frigate under us, it would be no contest. These Cyclone Mark II class vessels just have the tonnage or armor to stand up to her one on one. The Hall and the Newton are proof of that."

"Truth." Herc turned to the Brighton's helmsman. "Get us out of here. Maximum military speed!"

"Aye sir!" The helmsman kicked the Brighton's engines into overdrive and the small vessel lurched forward, gaining speed, as it bounced along the waves.

"Any sign of the Megalodon?" Herc barked at the ship's sonar tech.

"None," the petty officer answered.

Turning his attention to Weaver, Herc asked, "Let's assume for a moment that we do get out of here alive. . ."

"I would almost rather not, Captain," Weaver

flinched at the thought of the political horrors that lay ahead of them.

"How do we explain all this?" Herc shook his head. "The brass is gonna have our heads for losing the platform *and* two ships."

"Contact coming up on stern!" The sonar tech jumped out of his chair to his feet. "It's the Megalodon!"

"First things first," Weaver laughed darkly.

Funny, Herc thought, *I hadn't realized just how of a sarcastic jerk Weaver was before.*

Herc regretted the thought as soon as it had passed through his mind. He and Weaver had served together for years. It was uncalled for.

"The Megalodon is matching our speed, sir," the sonar tech said, taking his seat again. "She's not trying to ram us!"

"Lock onto it, but don't fire unless I give the order," Herc shouted at the gunnery officer. "No need to make it angrier than it already is."

Herc shot Weaver a look. "What do you make of that?"

"Could be she's injured as I suggested earlier or maybe she's just biding her time and playing with us."

"Options?"

"There are only two as I see things. Keep running like a bat out of Hell and hope she lets us go or engage her."

Herc walked around his command chair and plopped into it. "We run," he told Weaver.

"Petty Officer James, you keep a sharp eye on that screen of yours. If that thing out there changes course or increases speed, I want to know the instant it happens. You understand me?"

****

Minutes became hours as the Brighton continued on her course westward, away from the location of the remains of Sonar Platform 1. Herc shifted about uncomfortably in his chair, wishing the blasted Megalodon would make its move if it were going to. He couldn't understand why the thing would simply follow them. Why not attack outright and be done with the whole mess? The Megalodon had no reason to wait unless his XO was right and the thing *was* merely playing with them. He had seen cats do the same. Some animals like to torture their prey before ending its life, and this waiting was torture to him and his crew.

"James?" He asked.

"No change in the Megalodon's course or speed, sir. She's keeping her distance but staying with us."

Herc craned his neck to glance at where Weaver stood behind him. The XO looked as nervous as Herc felt. The nerve-wracking wait to see what Lightning had planned for them continued. Herc considered opening fire on the great beast, but if it was able to elude the torpedoes that he sent at it, the Brighton might not have time for a second volley before it was on them. Herc reached up, wringing the skin of his cheeks with the fingers of his right hand. There had to be a means to escape the situation they were in, but how? Radioing for help was out of the question. It was doubtful that any would be sent even if he did. The good Lord knew things were going to look bad enough to the press and his superiors as they stood. If help did come and still more ships were lost before the Megalodon was destroyed, it would just make things worse. Herc knew his career in the Navy was over. There was no coming back from a disaster on the scale of this one.

As if reading his thoughts, Weaver moved around beside him. "You've done everything you could and done it by the book as well."

"That's not going to save me." Herc lowered the hand he had been rubbing his face with and gripped the arms of his chair tightly. "How many people died today and for what?"

"If you get *us* out of this alive, that's enough for me," Weaver assured him.

"Thank you," Herc nodded at Weaver. "At this point, I'll take what I can get."

"Sir!" the sonar tech screamed. "The Megalodon is changing course. She's veering away from us, heading north!"

Hope flared within Herc. Maybe they were going to get out of this mess without a fight after all.

"Keep the engines at maximum," he ordered. Herc knew there was a chance they would burn out. He had pushed them to their limits already. Even so, the Megalodon was much faster in the water than the Brighton. Just because Lightning was veering away, didn't mean she couldn't return as fast as she had left. The question was whether this was a feint, or if the Megalodon was really deciding to let them go. Herc's instincts assured him that it wasn't likely to be the latter.

Herc and his bridge crew waited for the Megalodon to return. He had quit smoking some years ago, but right now, Herc would've traded just about anything for a cigarette. The storm was long gone. Stars filled the night sky. Their light was reflected on the surface of the ocean as the Brighton continued along its course. Another few hours and they would reach the Eastern Seaboard of the United States.

"Contact!" the sonar tech informed him. "The Megalodon is coming in at our port side! Speed forty knots and increasing!"

The ship's CIWS was active. As soon as it detected the giant shark closing in on the ship, the guns that were part of its system came to life, swiveling around to engage her. With a sound similar to that of a jet fighter breaking the sound barrier, the CIWS opened fire. The high caliber weapons spat a virtual wall of bullets outwards into the water where the shark had surfaced. Jagged wounds peppered the Megalodon's fin and exposed top side as the bullets ripped into the giant shark. The shark veered away from the Brighton, her speed reaching an astounding, sixty knots, as she fled the CIWS' onslaught.

"Yeah!" The Brighton's helmsman whooped, shaking a fist in the air.

"Let's save the elation until the battle is over," Herc cautioned the man.

Abashed, the helmsman dropped his head and refocused his attention on the controls in front of him.

"She's coming in again!" the sonar tech shouted.

The Megalodon's gigantic shape rose upwards from the ocean's surface once more. This time, the great beast was closing on the ship from behind. The CIWS' guns spun to meet her. Again, they erupted to life with a boom and poured a continuous stream of fire into the water. This time, Lightning didn't change course. Instead, she dove deeper into the waves, her fin vanishing from sight.

"Frag it!" Captain Herc Locklin cursed, smashing a balled up fist on the arm of his command chair. He knew what the sonar tech was about to yell at him before the man so much as opened his mouth. "She's under us!"

"Launch torpedoes!" Herc bellowed.

A volley swooshed from the Brighton's tubes. They were sonar guided and arced in their flight accordingly, zeroing in on the Megalodon. Seconds ticked away slowly as Herc waited for confirmation that they had found their target. He knew the shark was smart and fast enough to elude the torpedoes if luck was on its side.

"Negative contact!" the gunnery officer finally shouted.

Herc glanced at Weaver. "You're right. She's smart," he told the XO as he wondered just how the Megalodon had escaped the volley they had fired at her.

"There's a reef nearby," Weaver said. "She could have used it somehow to shake the torpedoes like a fighter pilot in a movie dodging a heat seeker."

"Don't suppose it matters how she did it as long as we hit her next time," Herc shrugged.

"Oh God," Herc and Weaver both heard the sonar tech mutter. Before the man could say anything else though, the Megalodon plowed into the Brighton from below her. The small frigate was tossed upwards, out of the water, before she splashed down, hard, back onto the waves. Weaver was knocked from his feet. His body slammed into the bridge wall with the sickening noise of cracking bones. Herc had clung to his command chair with all his strength or he might have suffered a similar fate.

The impact did a lot more than structural damage to the frigate. The Brighton's already heavily overtaxed engines blew. Alarm klaxons rang through the small ship as its systems kicked over to backup power. Herc counted them all blessed that the ship itself hadn't gone up with the engines.

Herc heard the helmsman scream as the controls in front of him exploded as a power surge ripped through them. The helmsman leapt from his seat and turned towards Herc before collapsing onto the deck. Herc saw that pieces of the shattered console were sunk into his forehead and cheeks, rivers of red running over the front of his uniform. The man's left arm was on fire and he waved it about wildly as he fell. The helmsman hit the deck with a thud and didn't move again. Another member of the bridge crew left their post and rushed over to help him.

Weaver wasn't in much better shape. The XO also lay on the deck. Herc could see that his collision with the bridge wall had broken Weaver's hip and most of the upper bones of his leg on the side of his body that had made contact. Two of Weaver's

79

fingers were bent unnaturally backwards, and they were stuck up above the rest of his hand, as the XO did his best to get up and failed.

"Medic!" Herc screamed but didn't dare leave his command chair himself to help the injured men. Lightning was still out there and it was up to him to stop her…somehow.

"Damage report!" Herc snapped.   Normally, Weaver would have been the one who answered but now it was the gunnery officer.

"We're on auxiliary power, sir!" the man told him. "There's massive damage to the hull and we're taking on water."

"Weapons?"

"The CIWS is offline. We've lost all but the aft torpedo tubes as well!"

"We've still got comms and most other systems are nominal," the sonar tech added.

"Where is she?" Herc barked at the tech.

"She's coming in again!"

"Take her with guns!"

The gunnery officer stabbed the firing mechanism for the aft launchers. A second volley shot outwards into the water to meet the oncoming Megalodon. "Torpedoes away!"

An explosion blossomed in front of the Brighton. The seeker torpedoes had swept back under the ship and had come around to strike their target. Huge splashes of water reached towards the heavens from the center of where they made contact with the giant shark. Herc smiled a feral smile as he leapt up from his seat to peer through the Brighton's forward window and saw that the water was tinted red.

"We got her," he growled.

"The Megalodon is still moving, sir!" the sonar tech warned him. "She's coming up under us again!"

"Brace for impact!" Herc bellowed, plunging back into his command chair and holding onto it for dear life.

The impact never came though. Herc shot a glance at the sonar tech.

"The Megalodon altered course sir. She's headed away from us...no, wait. She's swung about."

"Take her with guns!"

"Yes sir!" the gunnery officer answered as another volley of torpedoes sped forth from the Brighton's aft launchers. More explosions detonated out in the waters where the Megalodon lurked.

"The Megalodon's speed is now seventy knots, closing on our port side!"

"Holy. . ." Herc rasped as the Megalodon's impossible rate of speed registered in his brain. If she hit them this time, it was over.

"Empty the damn launcher!" Herc roared at the gunnery officer.

Three more volleys of torpedoes left the Brighton. Herc saw the sprays of water and blood from where the first volley struck the giant shark. The second followed within a heartbeat as their detonation was so close to the Brighton, he felt the shock waves rippling through the water underneath the damaged frigate.

Lightning's head rose above the water, her mouth open wide as she closed the last, small stretch of distance between her and the small ship. The final volley of torpedoes reached her in that moment. Her massive head disintegrated into bits of flesh and shredded tissue that spun away through the air from the rest of her body...and then the nightmare was over.

The uninjured members of the Brighton's bridge crew jumped to their feet, cheering and shouting, thankful to be alive. Herc rose from his command chair slowly and walked to the forward window. He stood at it for some time, staring at the swirling mass of crimson where the shark had been. Chunks of the Megalodon's burnt and torn apart body floated on the now calm surface of the water.

Herc gave the bridge crew a moment longer to celebrate before he returned to business. "Tell engineering I want the engines back online within the hour," he ordered, not caring if it were possible or not, "and break radio silence. I want medical relief here ASAP!"

The sun was rising on the distant horizon and Herc greeted it with a smile.

Epilogue

Dave clung to the side of his makeshift life raft as it drifted on the waves. The lift raft was little more than a floating piece of curved metal from the shattered hull of the USS Newton. The holding cell that the Newton's crew had tossed him into upon his arrival had saved his life. Its thick walls shielded him from the explosions that ripped the ship apart. In their wake, the door to his cell had been jarred open after the ship's main power went offline. Dave had escaped the sinking vessel before it went down. He wasn't a great swimmer by anyone's standards, but he had been able to keep his head above the surface long enough to find the jagged piece of the ship to which he now desperately clung to.

He had no supplies or even a weapon to defend himself with should one his sharks still be alive out there in the water somewhere. If one of *his* sharks survived, a weapon wouldn't make much difference anyhow.

Dave had tried to use his hands as paddles and steer his raft towards the still burning remnants of Sonar Platform 1 but failed. The platform was little more than a dot on the distant horizon as he dug through his soaked pockets, searching for something, anything that he could use to help him stay alive. His search came up empty.

The heat of the sun was amplified by the reflective surface of his raft. He was already sun burnt and blistered as he thought about how it all was such a waste. The nano-tech he'd spent years developing was gone. He had personally erased the files aboard the platform before taken from it as a hostage and the backup files he brought with him had been destroyed with the Newton.

Given the heat and lack of any means by which to obtain fresh water, Dave knew he didn't have much time left. There was always a chance that the cleanup crew that would surely be dispatched to wipe away any remaining evidence of his project might stumble onto him. Even if they did though, he half suspected they would put a bullet in his head. The sort of people in the government he worked for hated few things more than loose ends.

Dave looked out at the waves and saw the sharks coming. Their fins cut through the water, above its surface, at a speed impossible for a mere human to match. They weren't the great beasts he conducted his experiments on, but they would do the job all the same. As he watched them close in and begin to circle his makeshift raft, Dave burst into laughter. With all that had happened, somehow, this seemed the perfect way for his life to end.

Author Bio

Eric S Brown is the author of the Bigfoot War series, the Kaiju Apocalypse series (with Jason Cordova), A Pack of Wolves series, The Crypto-Squad series (with Jason Brannon), and the Jack Bunny Bam Bam series. Some of his stand-alone books include Kaiju Armageddon, Dawn of the Kaiju, Night of the Kaiju, World War of the Dead, The Weaponer, Last Stand in a Dead Land, and War of the Worlds Plus Blood Guts and Zombies. Two of his books have been made into feature films: Bigfoot Wars (Origin Releasing, 2014) and The Witch of Devil's Woods (Ingy Films, 2015). His short fiction has been published hundreds of time throughout the small press and beyond in such markets as Baen Books, The Grantville Gazette, and Walmart World Magazine. He also writes an ongoing pop culture column called, "Comics in a Flash." Eric lives in North Carolina with his wife and their two children.